Dear Parent:

Congratulations! Your child is taking the first steps on an exciting journey. The destination? Independent reading!

STEP INTO READING® will help your child get there. The program offers books at five levels that accompany children from their first attempts at reading to reading success. Each step includes fun stories, fiction and nonfiction, and colorful art. There are also Step into Reading Sticker Books, Step into Reading Math Readers, and Step into Reading Phonics Readers—a complete literacy program with something to interest every child.

Learning to Read, Step by Step!

Ready to Read Preschool–Kindergarten
• big type and easy words • rhyme and rhythm • picture clues
For children who know the alphabet and are eager to begin reading.

Reading with Help Preschool–Grade 1
• basic vocabulary • short sentences • simple stories
For children who recognize familiar words and sound out new words with help.

Reading on Your Own Grades 1–3
• engaging characters • easy-to-follow plots • popular topics
For children who are ready to read on their own.

Reading Paragraphs Grades 2–3
• challenging vocabulary • short paragraphs • exciting stories
For newly independent readers who read simple sentences with confidence.

Ready for Chapters Grades 2–4
• chapters • longer paragraphs • full-color art
For children who want to take the plunge into chapter books but still like colorful pictures.

STEP INTO READING® is designed to give every child a successful reading experience. The grade levels are only guides. Children can progress through the steps at their own speed, developing confidence in their reading, no matter what their grade.

Remember, a lifetime love of reading starts with a single step!

Copyright © 2004 Disney Enterprises, Inc./Pixar Animation Studios. Original *Toy Story* elements © 2004 Disney Enterprises, Inc. All rights reserved under International and Pan-American Copyright Conventions. Published in the United States by Random House Children's Books, a division of Random House Inc., New York, and simultaneously in Canada by Random House of Canada Limited, Toronto, in conjunction with Disney Enterprises, Inc. www.randomhouse.com/kids/disney

www.stepintoreading.com

Educators and librarians, for a variety of teaching tools, visit us at www.randomhouse.com/teachers

Library of Congress Cataloging-in-Publication Data
Jordan, Apple.
Buzz's backpack adventure / by Apple Jordan.
    p. cm. — (Step into reading. A step 2 book)

Summary: When Andy takes Buzz Lightyear to school, Buzz has an adventure in the midst of the classroom's outer space decorations.
ISBN: 0-7364-2209-9 — ISBN: 0-7364-8028-5 (alk. paper)
[1. Toys — Fiction. 2. Schools — Fiction.] I. Title. II. Series: Step into reading. Step 2 book.
PZ7.J755Bu 2004 [E] — dc21 2003008747

Printed in the United States of America   10 9 8 7 6 5 4 3

STEP INTO READING, RANDOM HOUSE, and the Random House colophon are registered trademarks and the Step into Reading colophon is a trademark of Random House, Inc.

DISNEY · PIXAR

TOY STORY AND BEYOND!

Buzz's Backpack Adventure

By Apple Jordan

Illustrated by Alex Maher

Random House 🏠 New York

Andy could not
wait for school.
Today was
space day!

"I will bring my space ranger, Buzz Lightyear," he said.

Buzz was excited.

He loved

space day!

In class, Andy learned about space.

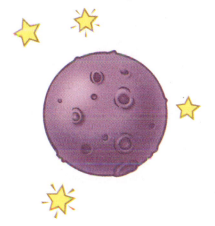 He learned about the stars and the moon.

He learned about the sun and the planets.

Brring!

The bell rang.

Lunchtime!

Buzz hopped out
of Andy's backpack.
He was ready
for fun!

Buzz saw the stars
and the moon.
He saw the planets.

Buzz could not
wait to explore.

Buzz saw
a hamster.
"Greetings,
strange creature,"
he said.

Buzz lifted the lid
to get a closer look.

Uh-oh!
The hamster
jumped out.
It ran off.

"Come back!"

Buzz cried.

"I mean you no harm."

Oops!

Buzz fell into

a jar of paint.

"Blast!" cried Buzz.
"I must clean
up and find
that creature."

Buzz looked for
the hamster
inside a desk.

Buzz saw old gum
and chewed pencils,
but no hamster.

Then Buzz met
some clay aliens.
He thought they
were space toys.

"Greetings,"
he said.
"Have you seen a
furry creature?"

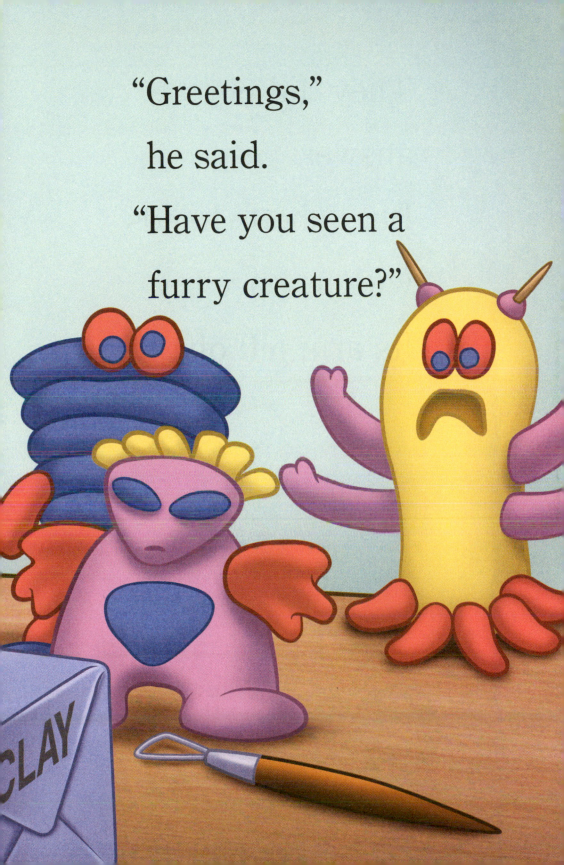

They did not
answer.
Buzz shook hands
with a space toy.
Its arm fell off.

"Sorry about that!"
Buzz cried.
He ran away.

Buzz landed on
a tower made
of blocks.

It wobbled

back and forth.

Crash!

At last it came

toppling down.

"Oh, no!" said Buzz. "I must clean up this big mess!"

"All done!" said Buzz.
Then the bell rang.
The class came
back from lunch.

Buzz hopped
into Andy's backpack.
No one saw him.

The class got ready
for show-and-tell.
Andy went first.

"This is Buzz,"
he said.
"Buzz is the BEST
space ranger ever!"